This
MOUSE ✹ WORKS
Classics Collection Storybook

belongs to

_____

Walt Disney's

ALICE
in
WONDERLAND

MOUSE WORKS

© 1993 Disney Enterprises, Inc.
Printed in the United States of America
ISBN: 1-57082-031-7
5 7 9 10 8 6 4

It was a very hot summer day. Not a cloud was to be seen, and not a single breeze disturbed the leaves or grass surrounding Alice's house.

"I'm so hot," Alice said, lifting up her long hair. She was perched in the crook of the big oak tree, singing to her cat, Dinah.

"Still, Alice, you must learn your lessons," her older sister said. "Now listen carefully." And Alice's sister began to read aloud.

Alice sighed. "In my own world, everything would be different," she whispered to Dinah.

Suddenly, a white rabbit ran by quite close to her.
Alice had never seen anything quite like it. The rabbit
actually wore a waistcoat, a red jacket and spectacles!

"Oh, dear! I'm late, I'm late, I'm late!" the rabbit said
to himself.

"Wait for me," Alice called as she jumped down from
the branch.

"I'm late for a very important date!" the rabbit said
without stopping to look at Alice. He took a very big
watch out of his waistcoat pocket. Alice ran across the
field after the rabbit.

"Where are we going?" she shouted, but the rabbit
didn't answer.

Alice followed him anyway,
but suddenly the rabbit
vanished. Alice was just in
time to see him pop down a
large rabbit hole under the
hedge.

Without thinking, Alice
followed the rabbit, jumping
down into the hole herself.
Her dress puffed up like a
balloon, and she fell and fell
and fell. "After this, I shall
think nothing of falling down
the stairs," she thought.

The hole was so deep, Alice
had lots of time to see what
was around her and to wonder
what was going to happen
next.

After a long fall, she
finally reached the bottom.

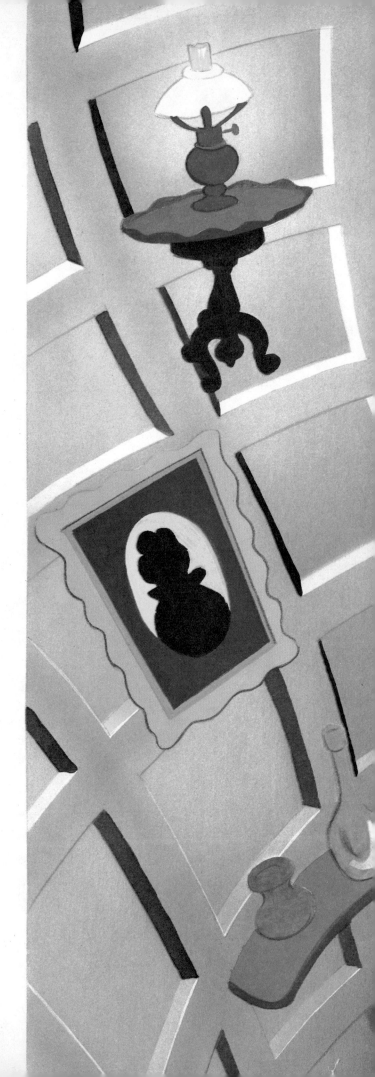

All Alice could see was a long tunnel in front of her.
Through the shadows, she could see the White Rabbit,
hurrying along ahead of her. "Oh, Mr. Rabbit! Wait,
please!" she cried. But the rabbit never looked back.

Alice tried to catch up with him. But when she turned
the corner, she found herself in a big hall, lit by lamps, but
with no windows. There was no sign of the White Rabbit.

Alice examined the hall
carefully and discovered a low
curtain. Behind it was a little
wooden door painted blue.

"Curiouser and curiouser,"
thought Alice. She knocked,
but no one opened the door.

"Mister Rabbit, will you
open the door?" she pleaded.

She tried looking through
the keyhole, and saw the White
Rabbit running through the
loveliest garden you could
ever dream about! She just
had to get there, so she
twisted the doorknob.

Suddenly, the doorknob
began to talk!

The doorknob guessed what Alice was thinking and said, "You're much too big, my dear. Why don't you try the bottle on the table?"

Alice looked around again and noticed that there was a table in the middle of the hall. She moved closer and saw a little bottle on it. Around the neck of the bottle, there was a label with the words "Drink me." Alice began to taste it and, as she liked it, she drank the whole bottle.

"What a strange feeling!" said Alice. She noticed that
she had become so tiny that she was now smaller than the
bottle on the floor beside her. The table looked gigantic.
Then she realized that now she would be able to get
through the little door.

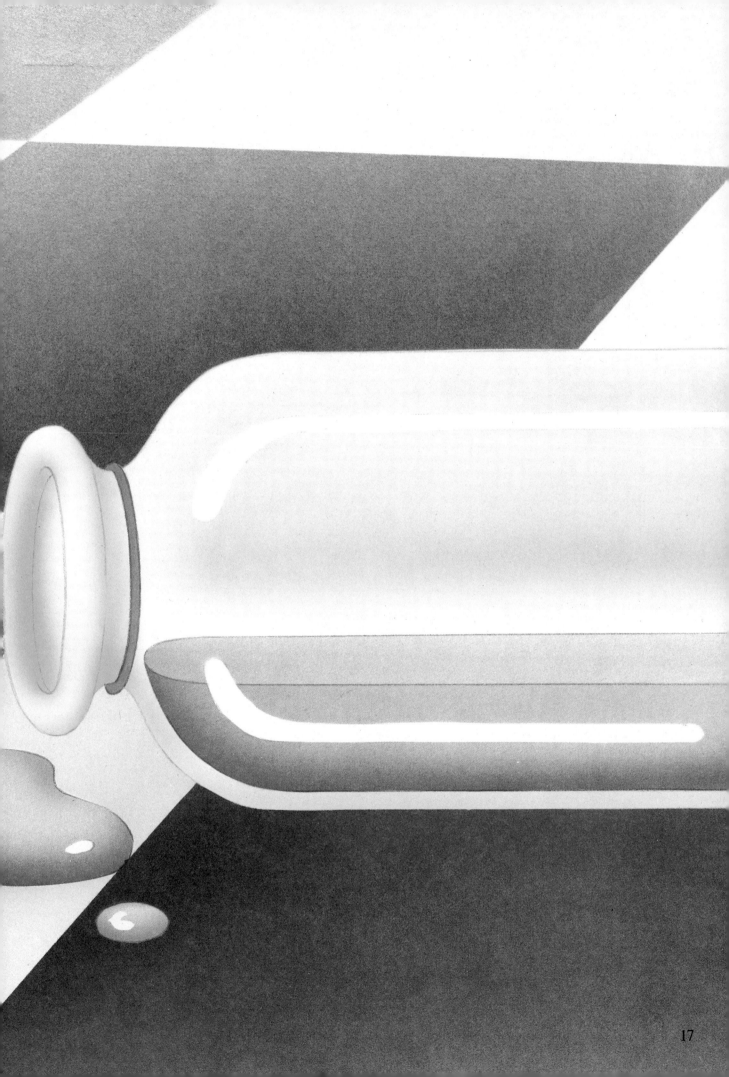

"Now I'm just the right size!" she told the doorknob.

"Yes, but I'm locked," he replied.

Sure enough, Alice discovered that she had left the key to the lock on the table, way out of reach. Alice tried her best to climb up one leg of the table, but it was too slippery. She was afraid she would never reach the key, when she noticed a box under the table. Inside was a small cake bearing the words "Eat me."

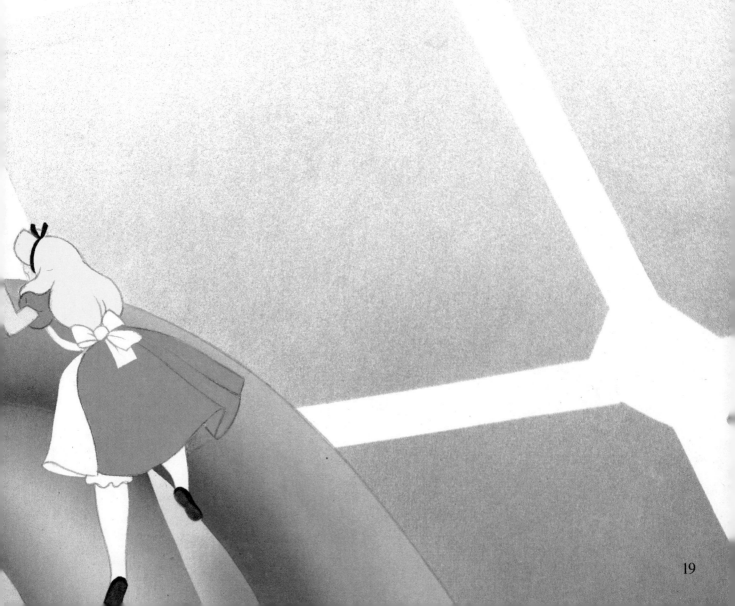

The cake tasted rather good, but when Alice looked at her hands, she saw them growing bigger and bigger.

"A little of that went a long way," laughed the doorknob.

But Alice didn't think it was very funny as her feet moved farther and farther away from her. The hall looked small and her head almost touched the ceiling. Alice had turned into a giant!

Alice realized that she was trapped in the room. "Now I'll never get home," said Alice, bursting into tears. She cried and cried and, since she was now a giant, she cried giant tears.

"You up there! Stop!" shouted the doorknob as the water began to rise.

Alice listened to this good advice. She drank what was left in the bottle, hoping to return to her natural size. Sure enough, she not only began to shrink, she soon was so small that the tears she had shed were like a salt-water ocean.

"I wish I hadn't cried so much," said Alice as she began floating toward the little door. Although the waves tossed her about, Alice knew how to swim and managed to reach the door.

27

On the other side of the
door, Alice was able to swim
to dry land. She looked about
her and said aloud, "I wonder
if that White Rabbit is around
here somewhere."

Two fat little men bounced toward her saying, "There isn't any White Rabbit here, but we are Tweedledee and Tweedledum, at your service!"

"I'm curious to know where the rabbit is going," Alice explained as the funny pair danced all around her.

But Tweedledee and Tweedledum didn't listen to what Alice had to say. All they cared about was talking and bragging.

"Shall we tell her a story or a poem?" Tweedledee asked.

"Let's have a poem. I'm sure she'll be delighted to hear our poem," Tweedledum decided.

Alice was still wondering about the White Rabbit, but she didn't know how to get away from the strange twins.

"'The Walrus and the Carpenter.' A poem written by Tweedledee and Tweedledum and by Tweedledum and Tweedledee," announced the two. They launched into a silly tale of a greedy Walrus and a Carpenter who lured a family of unsuspecting oysters to their table.

"That was a very sad story," said Alice, when they had finished.

But Tweedledum and Tweedledee began fighting about what poem to recite next, and Alice was able to slip away.

Alice was glad to get away from such silly fellows. She walked awhile and then came across a magnificent garden with beautiful flowers and fountains. Alice felt happy again as she saw a house in front of her. It was the most charming house she had ever seen. "I wonder who lives here," thought Alice.

Suddenly the shutters opened, and who should Alice see but the White Rabbit!

"Hello!" Alice shouted.

The rabbit came down and opened the front door, and he didn't seem at all surprised to see Alice. But instead of saying "hello," he began scolding her. "Mary Ann! What are you doing out there? Run inside this moment and fetch me a pair of gloves and a fan! Quick, now!" Without arguing, Alice ran into the house.

"He mistook me for his housemaid," she said to herself as she ran upstairs.

The inside of the rabbit's house was just as delightful as the outside. As Alice looked at the quaint pictures and furnishings, she heard the White Rabbit calling to her.

"Mary Ann! My gloves! I'll be late!"

"Oh, very well. Where did he put those gloves, anyway?" said Alice, as she searched the rabbit's chest of drawers. She found no gloves, but she did find a box full of cookies. They looked so appetizing, Alice could not resist tasting them.

She had barely finished
eating a cookie when she
found her head pressing
against the ceiling! Alice had
grown so big, she could no
longer fit in the house. Her arms
stuck out of the windows and her
feet stuck out of the doors.

She could hear the rabbit
yelling, "A monster! Help! There
is a monster in my house!"

39

No wonder the rabbit was frightened. Alice was as big as a giant now. In fact, she was so big, she couldn't move at all. "Good gracious! One can't eat anything here without changing like a telescope," Alice thought.

As she peered through the little window, she saw that a strange Dodo Bird had joined the White Rabbit. They began to discuss what had happened.

"How did the giant get into your house?" asked the Dodo.

"I don't know, but that's not the problem. How will we get him out?"

"I have a simple solution," said the Dodo. "We will smoke him out!"

The Dodo prepared to set the house on fire. As smoke began to climb toward her, Alice noticed a small garden outside the window, near her hand. She reached out and pulled, and there was a tiny carrot in her hand. The rabbit saw what she was doing and tried to stop her, but she managed to pop the carrot into her mouth. After all, she was getting used to growing and shrinking.

As soon as Alice had nibbled the carrot, she began to grow smaller once again.

Once she was small enough to get through the door, Alice ran out of the house. She saw that the dodo was very disturbed that she had ruined his plan. "No cooperation. No cooperation at all," he told the White Rabbit. It seemed that even though Alice was gone, he still wanted to burn the house down, but the rabbit talked him out of the plan.

Relieved of the worry about the giant in his house, the White Rabbit suddenly remembered his appointment. "I'm late, I'm late, I'm late!" he said as he ran off once again.

Alice hurried away from the rabbit's house, as well. Even though she was now so small that the grass seemed like a gigantic forest, Alice was happy to be free again. Then she realized that she had no idea where she was or how to get back home. "I guess I'll have to find the White Rabbit," she decided, heading in the direction where the rabbit had disappeared. "But when he notices he forgot his gloves, he'll be mad at Mary Ann. And since he thinks I am Mary Ann, he'll probably be mad at me!"

Alice noticed that her surroundings were not only
enormous, but they were very strange, as well. Bread-and-
butterflies fluttered all about her, and delicate rocking-
horseflies galloped through the air. There were even talking
flowers! Everything was so unusual here, Alice stopped
trying to figure things out. She was truly in a wonderland
in which everything was different from the world in which
she had lived. "I wonder if I'll ever get home again,"
sighed Alice, as she continued through the grass.

Soon Alice saw smoke rising out of the grass. It was coming from a small clearing. She stood on tiptoe and peeked over the top of a large mushroom. Her eyes met those of a large caterpillar, sitting on top of the mushroom with his arms folded, quietly smoking a long water pipe.

The Caterpillar looked at Alice, then took the pipe out of his mouth and spoke. "Who are you?" he asked, blowing big round smoke rings into the air.

"I hardly know, sir. I've changed so many times since this morning, you see," Alice answered.

The Caterpillar was irritated. "I do *not* see. Exactly what is your problem?"

"I should like to be a little larger," she told him.

"I tell you this. One side of the mushroom will make you grow taller and the other side will make you grow shorter." Saying this, the Caterpillar turned into a butterfly and flew away!

Alice looked thoughtfully at the mushroom for a while. "But which is which?" she wondered. It was a very difficult question.

She decided to take a chance. "I'm tired of being only three inches high," she said as she bit off a piece of the mushroom.

As soon as she did, she grew so quickly that her head pushed through the tops of the trees. Alice found herself looking out over the top of the forest, frightening the birds.

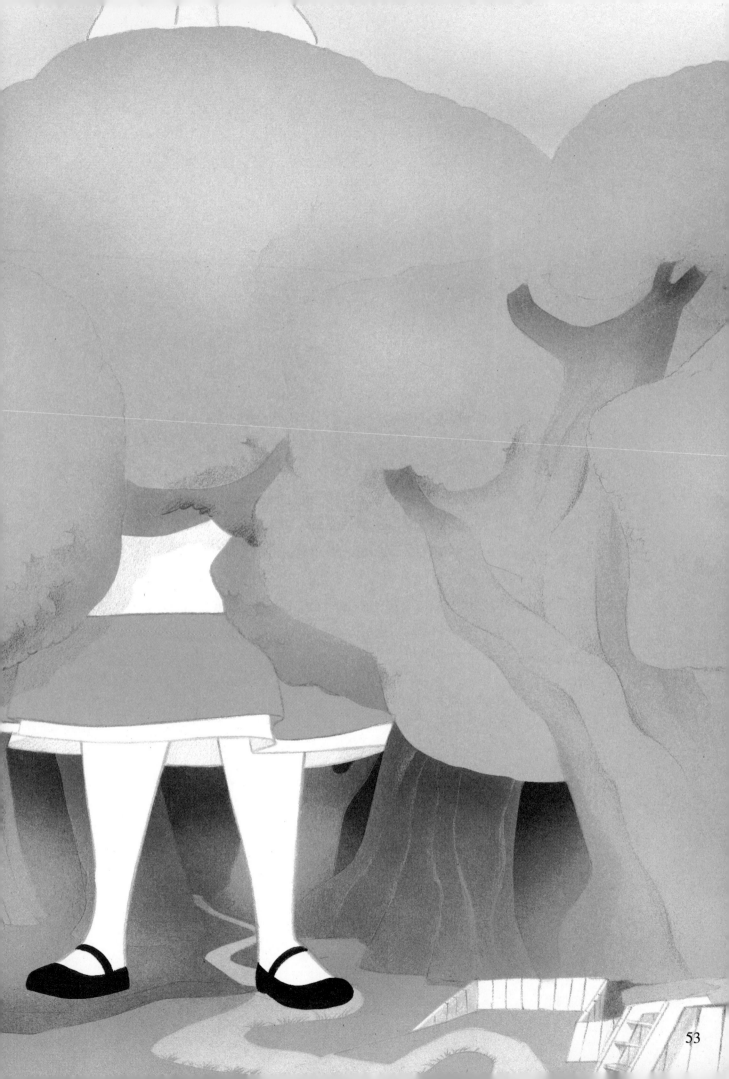

Alice had become a giant again! She could hardly see her feet. And while she was rising through the trees, a bird's nest with eggs in it had ended up on top of her head.

"Shoo! Shoo! Go away," shouted the angry mother bird, flapping around Alice's head. "Serpent! Go away!"

"I'm not a serpent. I'm just a little girl," Alice told the bird. The bird laughed. "Little!"

No matter what Alice said, she could not convince the bird that she was not a serpent and didn't want her eggs.

Alice found it exhausting to keep changing her size all
the time. She had had enough of being either a giant or
the size of an ant. "I wish I could go back to my real
size!" she said.

Then she remembered she still had pieces of the
mushroom in her pocket. So she nibbled at the bit of
mushroom she had kept and brought herself down to a
more normal height. She kept a piece, just in case she
might need it later.

"Who knows? Things are so very odd in this place,"
she thought.

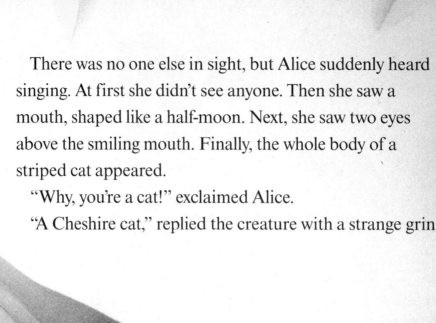

There was no one else in sight, but Alice suddenly heard singing. At first she didn't see anyone. Then she saw a mouth, shaped like a half-moon. Next, she saw two eyes above the smiling mouth. Finally, the whole body of a striped cat appeared.

"Why, you're a cat!" exclaimed Alice.

"A Cheshire cat," replied the creature with a strange grin.

"Would you please tell me which way I ought to go?" Alice asked the Cheshire Cat.

"That depends on where you want to go," said the Cat, who had an odd way of disappearing and then appearing again before Alice's eyes.

"But if you really want to know, he went that way," said the cat, pointing.

"Who?" Alice was very puzzled.

"The White Rabbit. If I were looking for him, I'd ask the Mad Hatter or the March Hare," replied the Cheshire Cat, disappearing once again. This time, he did not reappear.

"How very curious," said Alice, and she continued walking through the woods.

Soon she arrived at a clearing where a big table was all
set for afternoon tea. The March Hare and the Mad Hatter
were seated at the table. There were several teacups and a
large teapot full of hot tea and a big pink birthday cake.

As the March Hare was serving, the Mad Hatter greeted
her. "I'm sorry I interrupted your birthday party," said Alice,
politely.

"This is not a birthday party," said the Mad Hatter. "This is an
*un*birthday party."

"A what?" asked Alice.

The Mad Hatter explained that everyone has just one birthday
a year, but that we all have 364 unbirthdays.

Alice told him it was her unbirthday, too. The March Hare
and the Mad Hatter were delighted to help her celebrate.

Alice tried to enjoy the unexpected party. But even though it was a tea party, she never got any tea. The March Hare started to pour her some tea, but he bumped into the Mad Hatter, who spilled his tea on his coat and bow tie. They poured tea on each other and broke many teacups, but Alice still had nothing to drink.

There was also a sleepy Dormouse in the teapot, who recited a silly poem.

"This is the stupidest tea party I've ever been to," said Alice. "I'm going home."

The Mad Hatter and the March Hare were laughing so hard at their own jokes, they didn't notice that she had slipped away.

Alice continued walking through the forest, but once again, she didn't know which way to go. There were many confusing signs along the way.

"Which sign is right?" Alice wondered. It didn't take long for her to realize that she was hopelessly lost.

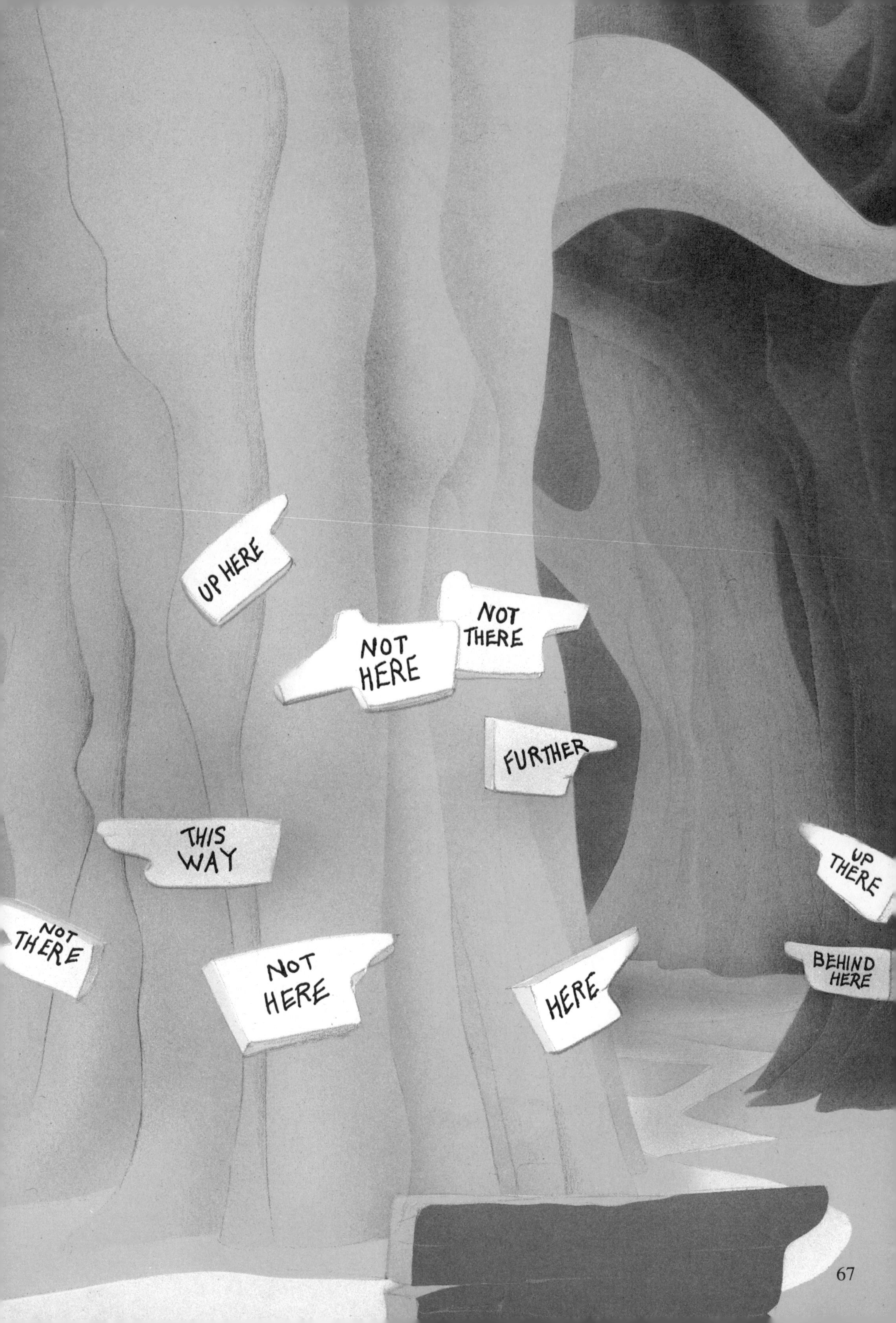
UP HERE
NOT HERE
NOT THERE
FURTHER
THIS WAY
UP THERE
NOT THERE
NOT HERE
HERE
BEHIND HERE

When she finally found a path to follow, Alice was sure that it would lead her home again. She was happy, until a strange creature came by. The animal had the body of a dog and the head and the tail of a broom. He swept everything in his way, including Alice's path. He swept all around her, erasing the path. When he left, there was no path left for Alice to follow.

"It's a good idea to stay where you are until someone finds you," Alice told herself. Suddenly, out of nowhere, the Cheshire Cat appeared in a nearby tree.

Alice told him that she wasn't looking for the White Rabbit any more. Now, all she wanted was to go home.

Still grinning, the Cheshire Cat told her he knew of a shortcut. He pointed the way. Soon Alice was happily skipping through the forest once again. This time, she was certain she would be back home very soon.

Alice found herself in a beautiful garden, with tall green hedges and pretty fountains. A large rose bush stood at the entrance to the garden.

There were three gardeners shaped like playing cards, who were busily painting the white roses red.

"Would you tell me," Alice asked timidly, "why you are painting the roses red?"

"Yes, Miss," answered one of the gardeners. "The Queen likes only red roses. And if she found out we planted white roses by mistake, she would have our heads cut off!"

Just at that moment, one of the gardeners, who had
been anxiously looking across the garden, called out "The
Queen! The Queen!" Alice heard the royal trumpeters. The
doors of the palace opened and a long line of soldiers
marched out. Like the gardeners, they were shaped like
playing cards, black and white or red and white.

Everyone stopped to watch the parade of palace guards, including Alice and the White Rabbit, who was one of the royal trumpeters. After the playing cards had passed, the Queen of Hearts approached, followed by her husband, the meek little King. Everyone seemed to be afraid of the Queen, including the King.

"Who's been painting my roses red?" bellowed the Queen. "Someone will lose his head!" The playing cards were very frightened.

The Queen stopped and stared at Alice. "And who is this?"

"I'm trying to find my way home," Alice explained.

The Queen asked Alice if she played croquet and was pleased to hear Alice reply that she played a little. "Then let the games begin," the Queen commanded.

And what a curious game it was, with live hedgehogs instead of balls and live flamingos instead of mallets.

The Queen loved the game of croquet, and she would do anything to win—even cheat. Every time the Queen hit the hedgehog, the crowd cheered.

Alice had a difficult time. Just as she got the flamingo's body tucked away and was about to hit the hedgehog with the bird's head, the flamingo twisted itself around and stared up at her face. Still, Alice managed to hit the hedgehog, which made the Queen very angry.

Then, out of nowhere, the Cheshire Cat appeared again. The Queen didn't see him as the cat playfully tied the hem of her dress to the flamingo's beak.

The Queen didn't notice what the Cheshire Cat had done. Just as she was about to win the game, she lifted her arms up high. When the flamingo held on to her skirt, the Queen toppled over. All that could be seen of Her Majesty were her legs wiggling in the air. Everyone had a good laugh, including her husband, the little King.

When the Queen finally got up, she was red as a lobster and she began to have a temper tantrum. She blamed Alice for everything that had happened to her.

By this time, of course, the Cheshire Cat had disappeared once again. Alice denied that she had played the trick, and tried to explain about the strange cat, but the Queen wouldn't listen. She was convinced that Alice had committed some kind of terrible crime.

"Off with your head!" the Queen screamed.

"She must be tried first,"
the King told her timidly. The
Queen was astounded that he
had dared to speak.
    "Then let the trial begin!"
ordered the Queen.

The Guards marched Alice to the courtroom right away. Alice was impressed when the Queen got up on a very high throne. She felt very small, indeed.

Then the Queen began the trial. "Off with her head!" she said. Alice was shocked at how fast the trial was moving along.

The shy little King said, "But that's not a trial, my dear. There must be witnesses. And a jury must decide what the sentence will be."

"Oh, very well. Hurry up, now. Let's get it over with," said the Queen. Alice sighed with relief.

However, the witnesses weren't much help. The Mad Hatter and the March Hare turned the courtroom upside down with their silly songs. Alice knew that if she wanted to get out of this terrible situation, she would have to take care of herself. The little King could not help her any more.

As the strange trial continued, she thought and thought. Then she realized that she still had some of the mushroom in her pocket.

"All I have to do is eat some of the mushroom and I'll be very big again. That will scare them off!" She bit into the mushroom and started growing right away.

Everyone in the courtroom went into a panic when Alice became a giant. As the Guards rushed toward the exit, the Queen shouted, "All persons over a mile high must leave the courtroom!"

"Who cares what you say?" asked Alice. "You're nothing but a pack of cards!" The Queen was horrified to see Alice pick up her Guards and drop them one by one.

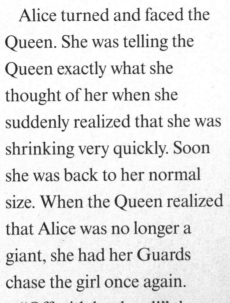

Alice turned and faced the Queen. She was telling the Queen exactly what she thought of her when she suddenly realized that she was shrinking very quickly. Soon she was back to her normal size. When the Queen realized that Alice was no longer a giant, she had her Guards chase the girl once again.

"Off with her head!" the Queen of Hearts kept shouting. Even the King was chasing Alice now.

But Alice ran as fast as she could, and she finally found a door and escaped.

Just when she thought she was safe, Alice discovered that she was trapped in a maze. She could hear the pounding feet of the Guards searching for her. "How will I ever find a way out?" she wondered. Suddenly, all she wanted to do was give up and go to sleep.

Alice could still hear the Queen's voice, shouting in the distance, but the sound was faint now. When she looked back, she saw the Mad Hatter, the March Hare, the White Rabbit, and the Queen of Hearts all chasing her. But now they seemed to be far behind. It was almost as if they were floating in a cloud. Their voices sounded very far away, and they all seemed to be calling her name: "Alice! Alice!"

"Wake up, Alice. You've been sleeping a
long time!" Alice's sister gently shook her awake.

"I've had such a strange dream!" said Alice. "I followed
a White Rabbit who was wearing a waistcoat and I ended
up in a Wonderland with a Cheshire Cat and the Queen of
Hearts!"

"Of course you did," said her sister, smiling, as they
walked back home for tea.